# The Story of the
# Little Piggy
# Who Couldn't
# Say No

Sabine Ludwig · Sabine Wilharm

# The Story of the Little Piggy Who Couldn't Say No

Sky Pony Press
New York

The day is lovely with bright sun.
A swim, thinks piggy, would be fun.
With swim tube, ball, her book, and hat,
and beach towel—must remember that—
she takes a tasty snack and drink,
gives Mom a good-bye wave and wink.
But Momma wants a kiss good-bye.

The bus has left! She breathes a sigh.

But walking's healthy too, she knows.

So no complaining, off she goes.

Here comes a dog. He's really quick.

"That tube, I want it now. No trick!"

No, piggy thinks, it cost a lot.

To her this seems to be a plot.

"Think it'll pop?  That's all that matters?"

His laughter stops. The tube's in tatters.

Without her swim tube, on she goes.
But kitty cat waves at her nose,
"Stop! Wait! I need to go to town
to buy some worms, but folks will frown
at me like this. Lend me your hat.
'Cause you don't look so good in that!"

"But I need holes to fit my ears."
Thwack! Thwack! is what the piggy hears.

The pig plods on.  Her head is bare.
She cheers up in the nice fresh air.
"Give us your ball!" She hears the scream
of rabbits from the soccer team.
They shoot and dribble, they attack.
"If I could just get that ball back!"
she sighs. She'd get it if she could.

She hears the call of beach and sea,
and crying too. Who can it be?
The croc sheds every tear she's got
and yammers, "I don't need a lot.
Your glasses, please, give them to me."

Pig squints, eyes burn, it's hard to see.

"Hey, piggy, heading through the wood?
Another cookie would be good.
But my bag's empty. I want more.
Do you have one—or three or four?"
The badger takes the cookie sack.
"Wow, these are great!" He holds it back.

He smacks his lips, eats all she had.
No more left? So what? Too bad.

Oh well, thinks pig, I smell the sea.

But bear's as noisy as can be!

**"Help, help!"** he cries loudly.

"I'm stuck in this bog.

The honey was yummy, but in a weak log.

Take your towel, give me a hand,

Pull hard, and get me on dry land."

"You'll soon be out, so hold on tight!"
The piggy pulls with all her might.

...ears apart.

**"Yikes!"** yells the bear with quite a start.
But worse, for pig, with splash and whomp
she also plops right in the swamp.

The others laugh, have no regret
at seeing pig get soaking wet.

This is just too much.

The pig screams, **"NO!"**

The rest, they look quite sheepish, though.

"Full of cheer, I left today
to swim, but things are not okay!
I'm in this mud, I'm really stuck.
Stop laughing at my rotten luck!
I helped you all, now don't you see?
Please grab hold and pull on me!"

**"Hey!"**

Shouts the bear. "Don't run away!
"I've been stuck in this all day."

Bear grabs the pig and won't let go.
It's too much for the others, so

they topple, tumble, fall, and kick

over stone and root and stick

into the mud, head over heels.

The gunk goes splat, the piggy squeals,

"This mud bath is the best, you know.

Let's get messy, head to toe!"

They romp and splish and splash away
till no mud's left in which to play.
The sun goes down, dark is the land,
the moon shines on the little band.
They start to yawn, a tummy growls.
"I need to eat!" the big bear howls.
A mouse would please the cat a lot.

"Let's go home!" So off they trot.

"Good night, little pig, till tomorrow at ten,
then all of us will go swimming again."
"I'll bring us a swim ring!" "And I'll have a hat!"
"Bake cookies?" "The badger is real good at that."
So those are the things her friends suggest,
But piggy is tired. She just wants to rest.

Her mother asks, "Have fun, my sweet?
Your dinner is ready. Come in and eat."

Library of Congress Cataloging-in-Publication Data is available on file.
ISBN: 978-1-62087-684-8
Manufactured in China, January 2013
This product conforms to CPSIA 2008